That's

GW00994396

Illustrations by
Strawberrie Donnelly

EGMONT
(children's books)

First published in Great Britain 2000 by Egmont Children's Books Limited
239 Kensington High Street, London W8 6SA
Illustrated by Strawberrie Donnelly
Text by Anna Ludlow. Designed by Phil Powell.
Copyright © 2000
ISBN 0 7497 4182 1
Printed in Italy

1 3 5 7 9 10 8 6 4 2

Sarah has come to play with Molly.
"Molly, show Sarah your toys," says Mum.

"Can I play with your doll?" asks Sarah.
"No, you can't," says Molly.

"Why not?" asks Sarah.
"She's mine!" says Molly.

"Can I play with your teddy?" asks Sarah.
"No!" says Molly. "He's **mine**."

"I let you play with my toys," says Sarah.
"But Teddy is tired," explains Molly.

"What about your baby animals?" asks Sarah.
"They don't like playing," says Molly.
"They usually do," says Mum.

"But I don't want anyone to play with them. They're **mine!**" shouts Molly.

"Why don't you build a house for the toys?" says Mum to Sarah.
"Yes, please!" shouts Sarah.

"But what about me?" cries Molly.
"There are enough bricks for both of you,"
says Mum, gently.

"What's that?" asks Lou.
"They're houses," says Molly proudly
to her little sister.

'But they look silly!" laughs Lou.

"We don't have enough bricks," whispers Molly.

"You could put this door there,"
whispers Sarah.

"Yours needs some windows at the front,"
whispers Molly.
"Then they won't look so silly," she says.

"Shall we build one
big house for the toys, now?"
suggests Molly.

"Oh, yes! A big house for all of them!"
says Sarah.
"That won't look silly at all!"

"Oooh, I like your new house!" says Lou.

We did it together!